For
Thomas and Daniel

BADLY DRAWN DOG by Emma Dodson

British Library Cataloguing in Publication Data

A catalogue record of this book is available from the British Library.

ISBN 0340 87806 1 (HB)
ISBN 0340 87807 X (PB)

First edition published 2005

10 9 8 7 6 5 4 3 2 1

Published by Hodder Children's Books,
a division of Hodder Headline Limited,
338 Euston Road, London, NW1 3BH

Printed in China

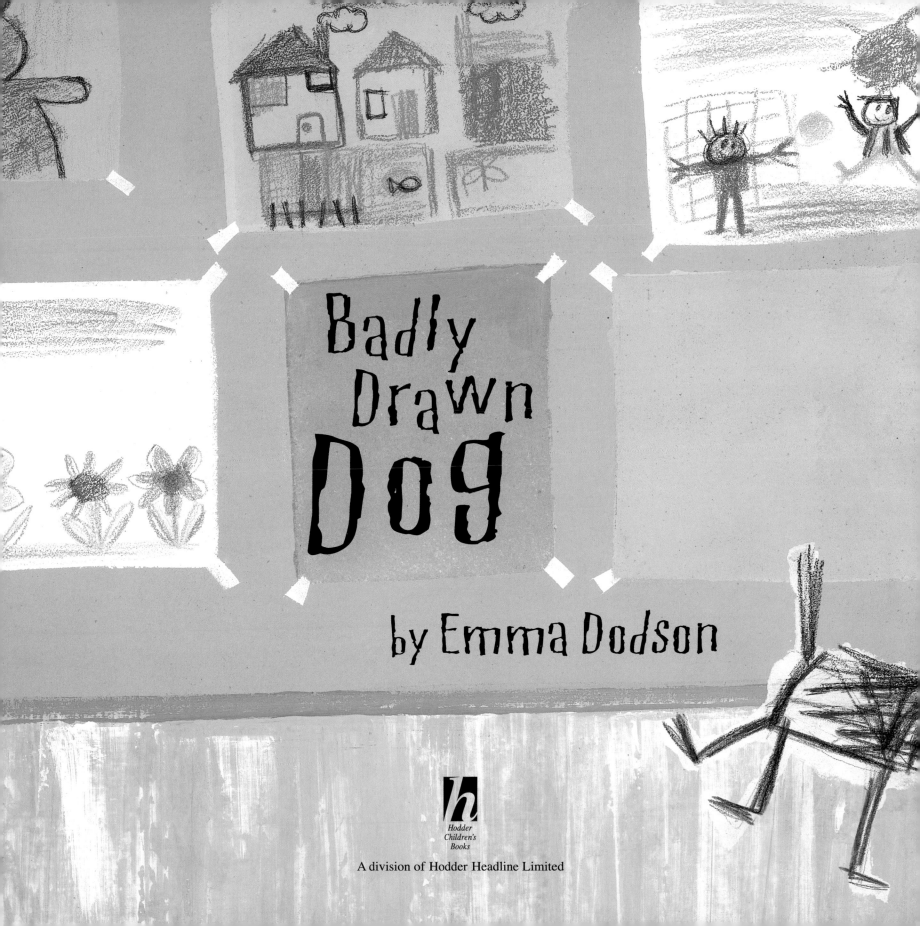

Badly
Drawn
Dog

by Emma Dodson

Hodder
Children's
Books

A division of Hodder Headline Limited

BADLY DRAWN DOG woke up one morning,
looked at his reflection and decided he was
tired of being badly drawn.

He was scribbly, scrawly and sketchy
round the eyes.
He looked like one big smudge.

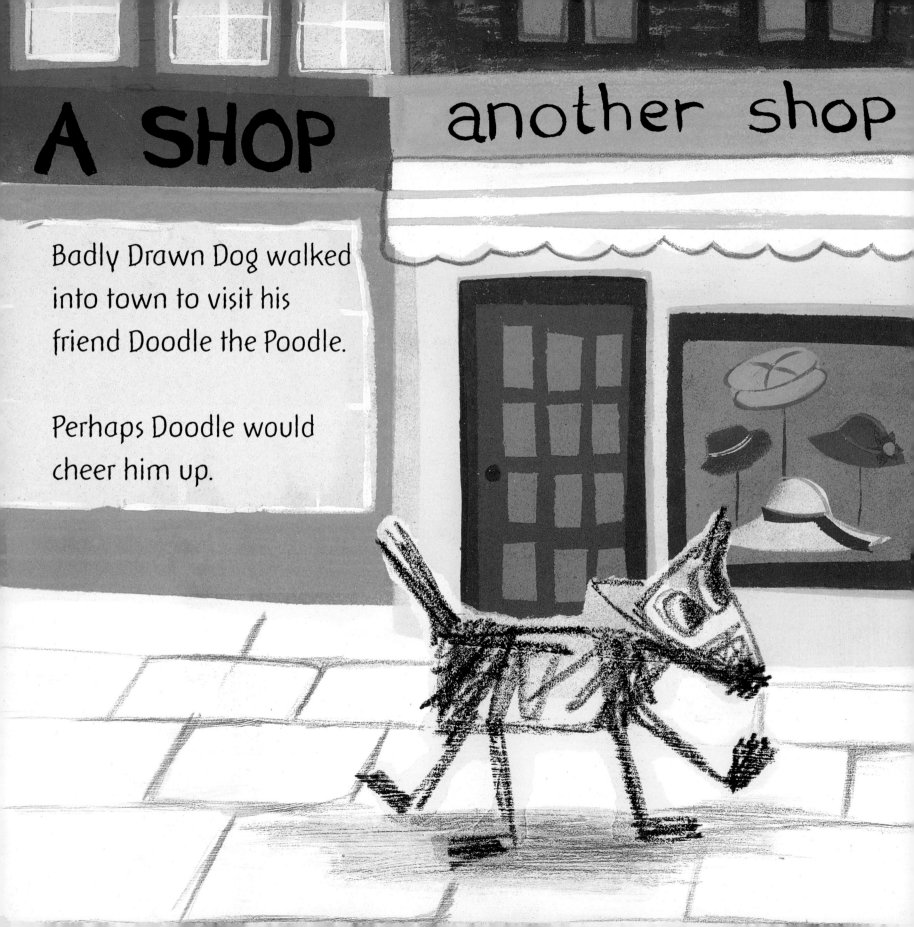

A SHOP

another shop

Badly Drawn Dog walked into town to visit his friend Doodle the Poodle.

Perhaps Doodle would cheer him up.

Then the artist set to work...

Badly Drawn Dog stared at himself in the mirror.

The artist said, 'Monsieur, you look marvellous, fabulous, wondrous, glorious, gorgeous.'

Badly Drawn Dog thanked him...

...and continued on his journey to see Doodle the Poodle.

All of a sudden

BANG!

SPLAT!

He walked straight into a lamp-post.

These eyes may take some getting used to, he thought.

Further on, Badly Drawn Dog saw two boys playing. He wanted to join in. When the ball bounced towards him, Badly Drawn Dog kicked it as hard as he could – The ball burst.

POP!

His new feet were too sharp.
The children were very sad.

And Badly Drawn Dog felt terrible!

Badly Drawn Dog went back to the artist and explained about the problems with his new style. He asked if he could be painted in something less pointy and sharp and with his eyes in the usual place, please.

The artist thought for a moment and set to work.

Artist's Studio

The artist did everything Badly Drawn Dog asked.

He said Badly Drawn Dog was now remarkable, incredible, beautiful, wonderful, phenomenal and très dazzling.

Badly Drawn Dog felt happier and set out again for Doodle the Poodle's house.

When he got there, Doodle the Poodle
opened the door and gasped!

Then he quickly slammed it shut.

Badly Drawn Dog shouted through the letterbox,
'It's me, Badly Drawn Dog. Open up, Doodle you Noodle!'

Doodle peered suspiciously from his window. 'What have you done to yourself? You're just a lot of blobs and swirls.'

'Don't you think my new
look is dazzling?' asked
Badly Drawn Dog.

'Errr yes,' said Doodle.
'but you hurt my eyes.
I'd better go.'

Badly Drawn Dog returned to the artist once again and asked if it would be possible to be painted in a less dazzling way – perhaps something a bit more normal.

Such a fussy fido, the artist exclaimed, and grumpily picked up his paintbrush.

When he had finished, Badly
Drawn Dog looked in the mirror.

'I really like this one,' he said.

'Yes, it is very popular,'
the artist agreed.

Badly Drawn Dog
decided to go home.

Soon he saw a dog
that looked just like him.

Then he saw another...

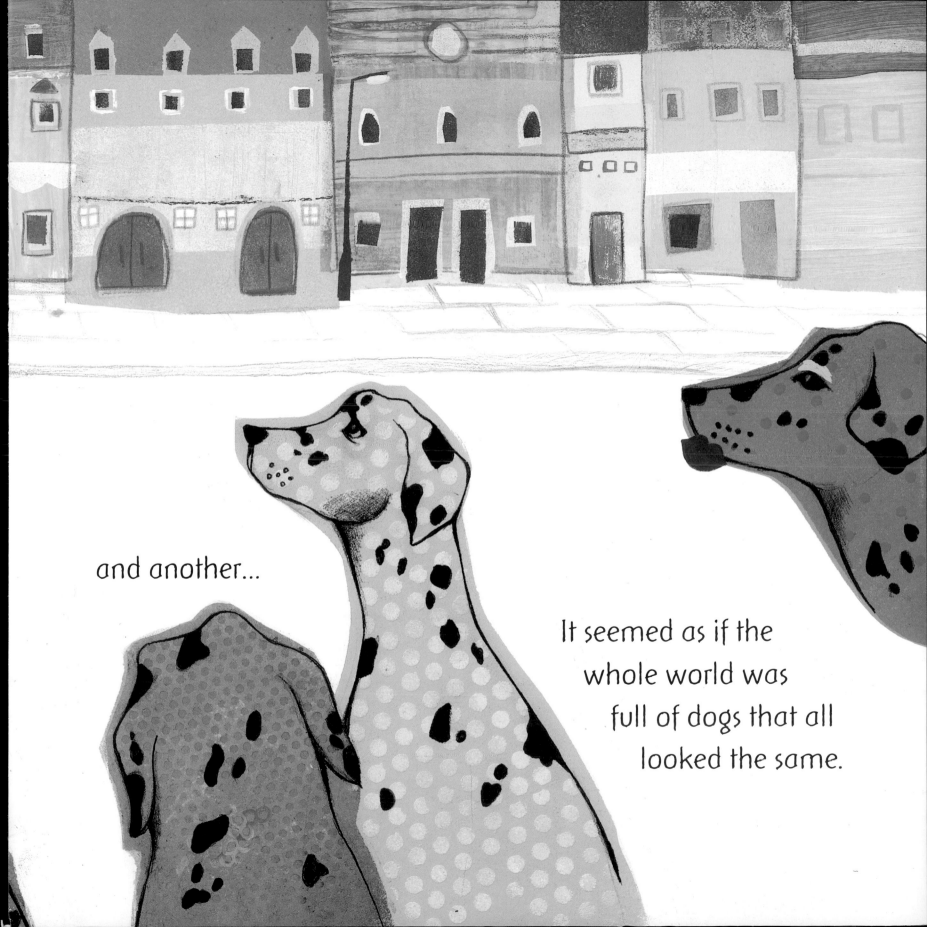

and another...

It seemed as if the whole world was full of dogs that all looked the same.

When Badly Drawn Dog reached his house
he found Doodle waiting for him.

'What do you think of my new popular look?'
he asked Doodle.

'I saw fifteen dogs who looked like you on my
way here,' Doodle replied. 'I liked you when you
were scribbly, scrawly and sketchy round the eyes.
You were one big friendly smudge.'

Badly Drawn Dog was disappointed.

'I know how we could get you back to being Badly Drawn, if you want,' said Doodle helpfully.

And he took Badly Drawn Dog back
to the little girl who created him.

She scribbled and scrawled and sketched
until he was his old self again...

...one big friendly smudge!

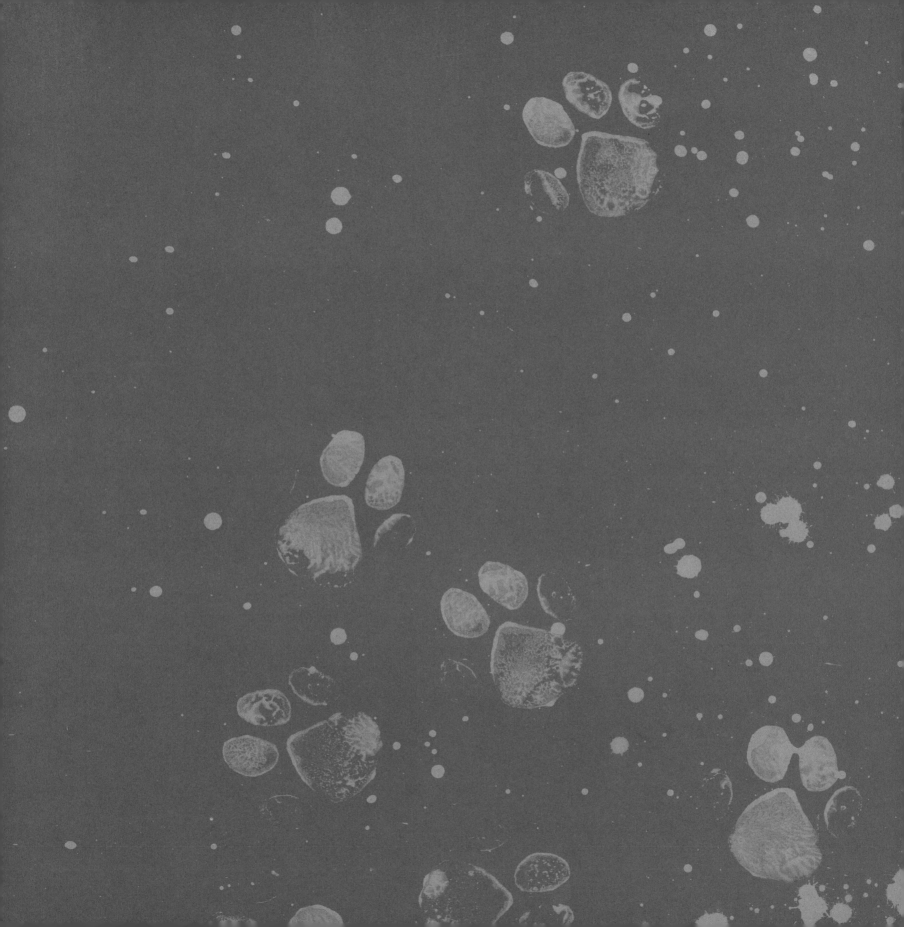